"*Letter from the Queen* is the book my young rural queer self needed. The story about owning what makes you special and finding the power to be your best 'you' is needed not only for queer kids, but all kids that feel marginalized and othered. Tara's experience as a storyteller shaped her book into a gorgeous read-aloud for all ages."

Calvin Crosby
Executive Director Brain Food Books
Co-Owner of The King's English Bookshop

"Embracing the beauty of individuality, Tara Lipsyncki weaves a tale of self-acceptance that resonates with queer readers young and old. A delightful celebration of being true to oneself. A must-read for nurturing self-confidence and healing your inner child."

Jonathan Hamilt
Executive Director of Drag Story Hour

Letter From The Queen

Written by Tara Lipsyncki   Illustrated by Cherry Mock

Letter from the Queen
Copyright 2023

Cover design © 2023 by Cherry Mock and Tara Lipsyncki
Cover designed by Cherry Mock

Ben was a special boy with hazel eyes and blonde **hair**. But people always told him, "You need to man up. You have way too much **flare**."

He was told to play sports, go camping, and get dirt on his **knees**.

To play rough and be manly. Always reminded, "Your emotions shouldn't be **seen**."

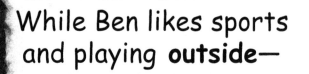

While Ben likes sports and playing **outside**—

He also likes outfits that sparkle, and he loves learning to **glide**.

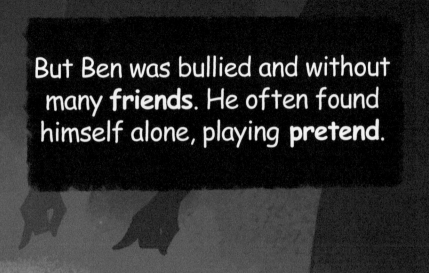

But Ben was bullied and without many **friends**. He often found himself alone, playing **pretend**.

Often, in his room late at **night**, he would cry in his pillow.

Little did he know about the magical gift he would get later that **night**. A gift so wonderful and fabulous, it would bring him pure **delight**!

When he woke up, sitting right there was a sight to be **seen**. A big glittery envelope, inside a letter from the **queen**!

"HEY BEN!
I WANTED TO TELL YOU
SOME SECRETS TO HELP
YOU THROUGH THE DAY.
THE FIRST ONE IS YOU'RE
SO MUCH MORE
WONDERFUL AND GIFTED
THAN MOST PEOPLE SAY!"

You're unique, and you're talented. You're brave and have a heart that is **true**. There are people in this world who love you for just being **you**.

Things may seem dark and hard to handle **right now**. You will never know how much I wish I could make all your problems magically disappear **somehow**.

Your life will be an adventure, filled with so much love and **glee**.

But the adventures only start once you let yourself be **free**.

Those things that people tease you about now—you know, the sparkle and **gliding**? Those will be the talents that will make your life so **exciting**!

You'll travel the world, find true love, and own lots of **puppies**. You'll make so many friends and host amazing themed **parties**.

It's ok to be **bold**, it's ok to
be different, but most of all,
it's ok to sparkle like **gold**.

And above all else remember who
you **are** and never forget that
home is never really that **far**.

Ben's mom walked in and couldn't believe what she was **finding**.

You see, for the first time in a long time, Ben was **smiling**.

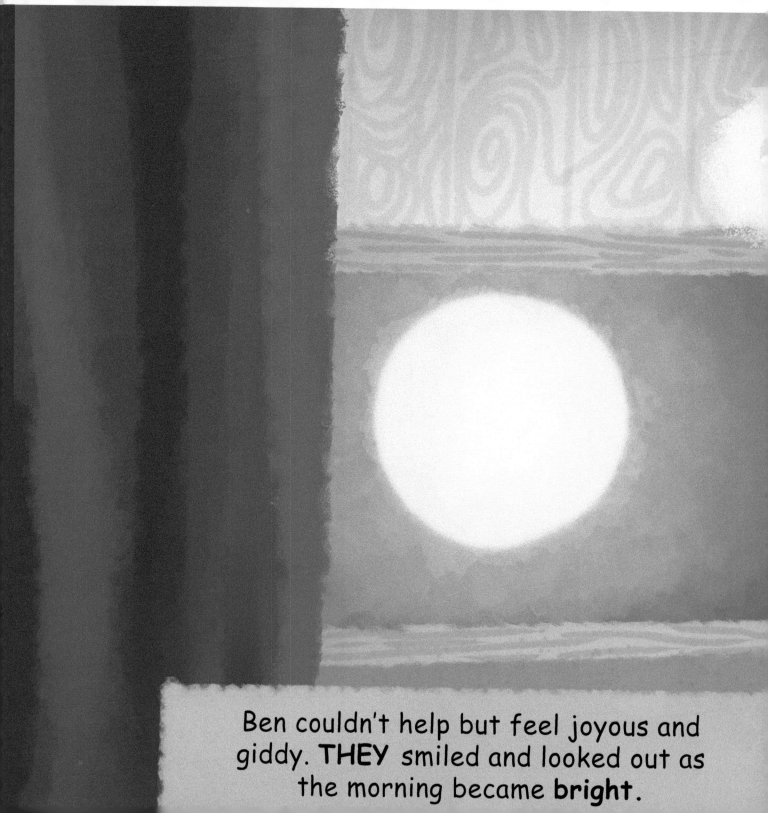

Ben couldn't help but feel joyous and giddy. **THEY** smiled and looked out as the morning became **bright**.

HEY READER,
NEVER BE AFRAID
TO WRITE YOUR OWN

HAPPILY EVER AFTER.

♡ TARA LIPSYNCKI